This book belongs to:

....

....

For Grandad
C.C.

For Mum with love xx
J.McC.

Reading Consultant: Prue Goodwin, Lecturer in literacy and children's books

ORCHARD BOOKS
338 Euston Road, London NW1 3BH
Orchard Books Australia
Hachette Children's Books
Level 17/207 Kent Street, Sydney NSW 2000

First published in 2011 by Orchard Books
First paperback publication in 2012

Text © Catherine Coe 2011
Illustrations © Jan McCafferty 2011

ISBN 978 1 40830 684 0 (hardback)
ISBN 978 1 40830 692 5 (paperback)

The rights of Catherine Coe to be identified as the author and
Jan McCafferty to be identified as the illustrator of this work
have been asserted by them in accordance with the
Copyright, Designs and Patents Act, 1988.

1 3 5 7 9 10 8 6 4 2 (hardback)
1 3 5 7 9 10 8 6 4 2 (paperback)

Printed in China

Orchard Books is a division of Hachette Children's Books,
an Hachette UK company.

www.hachette.co.uk

The
Best Friend
Boom

Written by **Illustrated by**
Catherine Coe **Jan McCafferty**

ORCHARD

Casper the Kid Cowboy was very excited. He had just heard about a lasso competition at the rodeo. The rodeo was where everyone went to show off their cowboy skills.

Yee-ha!

Casper had never won a competition before. But maybe he could win this one!

"You have to enter, Casper," said his best friend, Pete. "You can catch anything with your lasso!"

Pete was right. Casper liked to swing his lasso all day. He would catch trees, fences . . .

. . . and even Pete's hat!

Casper couldn't wait until he was old enough to have his own cattle ranch. Then he could use his lasso to control his cows.

"But the competition is on Saturday," Casper told Pete. "It's only three days away!"

"Don't worry, I'll help you practise!" Pete said to Casper. And so Casper spent the next three days, from morning till night, swinging his lasso.

Pete tried to help . . .

. . . but he wasn't very good.

At last it was Saturday. Pete
came over extra early. "Howdy,
Casper," he said.
Casper was nervous, but he tried
not to show it. "Howdy, Pete!"

There were lots of other
cowboys and cowgirls at the
rodeo. They all looked *very*
good at swinging their lassos.

"Oh dear," muttered Casper.
He felt very small and nervous.

But then his name was called,
and Casper had no more time
to worry.

Pete gave him a big cheer
and Casper rode into the ring.
He tried to look strong and
confident.

As soon as Casper started spinning his lasso, he forgot about his nerves.

He caught everything perfectly!

Everyone clapped when Casper had finished. He had never felt so happy.

Pete was very proud of his best
friend. The other cowboys and
cowgirls were good, but he
really wanted Casper to win.

It was time for the winner to be declared. Who would it be? "You were the best!" said Pete.

When Casper's name was read out, everybody cheered. Casper couldn't believe it. He'd won! "Howdy, folks! Thank you!" he said, as he collected his trophy.

As Casper left the rodeo, lots of people ran up to ask for his autograph.

Casper felt famous!

Casper was amazed. He had so many new friends! And he seemed to have forgotten about his oldest friend, Pete. "Hey, Casper! Wait for me!" Pete shouted.

But Casper didn't wait. He
was the lasso champion and
now *everyone* wanted to be
his friend.

Casper rode around with his new friends. They wanted to see his lasso tricks and hold his trophy.

"Yee-ha!" Casper shouted as he swung his lasso. But something was missing. Where was Pete? His best friend was nowhere in sight.

"Pete, where are you?" Casper shouted.

Casper looked at his new
friends, and then at his loyal
horse, Blue the Brave. He knew
what he had to do.

Casper galloped to Pete's ranch as fast as he could. Pete was outside, trying to lasso a tree.

"What are you doing here?"
Pete asked. "Where are all
your new friends?"
Casper began swinging his
lasso, and hooked it perfectly
over Pete's hat.

"They're not my *real* friends,"
Casper told Pete. "You're my
best friend. I'm sorry I left
you behind."

Pete smiled at Casper.
"Yee-ha!" Pete said.
"Yee-ha, partner!" said Casper.

Written by **Illustrated by**
Catherine Coe **Jan McCafferty**

All priced at £4.99

Orchard Books are available from all good bookshops,
or can be ordered from our website: www.orchardbooks.co.uk,
or telephone 01235 827702, or fax 01235 827703.

Prices and availability are subject to change.